Where the Girls Are

©1994 Annick Press Ltd. (North American edition)
©1993 Beltz Verlag, Weinheim und Basel (original edition)
Translation: A.W. Millyard

Annick Press Ltd.

Canadian Cataloguing in Publication Data

Heidelbach, Nikolaus
Where the girls are

Translation of: Was machen die Mädchen?
ISBN 1-55037-974-7

1. English language – Alphabet – Juvenile literature.
I. Title.

PE1155.H4513 1994   j823'.914   C94-930765-3

Distributed in Canada by:
Firefly Books Ltd.
250 Sparks Ave.
Willowdale, ON
M2H 2S4

Published in the U.S.A. by Annick Press (U.S.) Ltd.
Distributed in the U.S.A. by:
Firefly Books Ltd.
P.O. Box 1325
Ellicott Station
Buffalo, NY 14205

Printed in Canada by
Metropole Litho Inc.

Nikolaus Heidelbach

Where the Girls Are

Annick Press Ltd.
Toronto • New York

lison enjoys a sandwich.

Bridget is going out.

Charlotte sets a trap.

Deirdre trains for a career.

Edith performs a story.

Frances is sound asleep.

ertrude takes vacation photos at home.

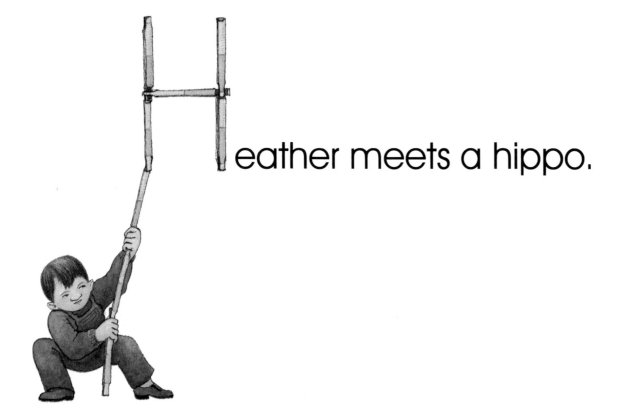

eather meets a hippo.

Iris doesn't wish to be disturbed.

Judith weds in secret.

Kim, Karen and Katharine look after their birds.

Louise drives in a race.

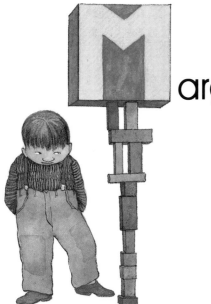

argaret receives a visitor.

Norma tickles Nadine.

lga works on her shot.

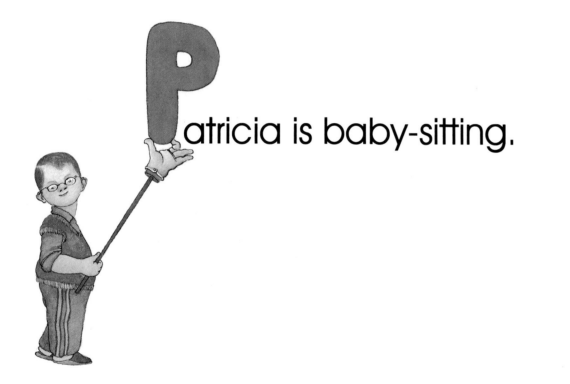

Patricia is baby-sitting.

 Queenie is doing the laundry.

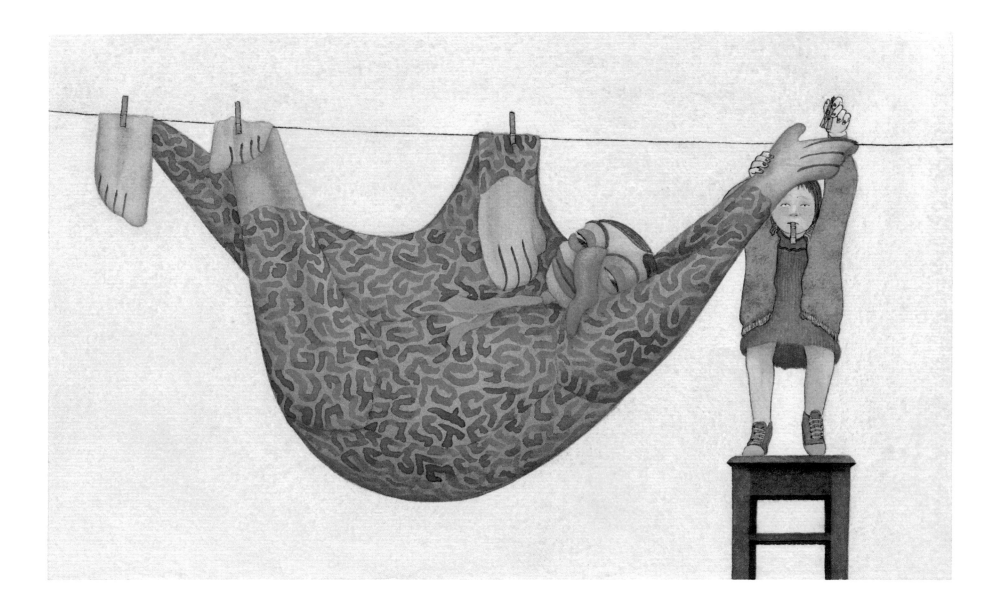

Ruth plays in a band.

ybil is freezing.

Tabitha helps her sister.

Ursula gets ready for a costume ball.

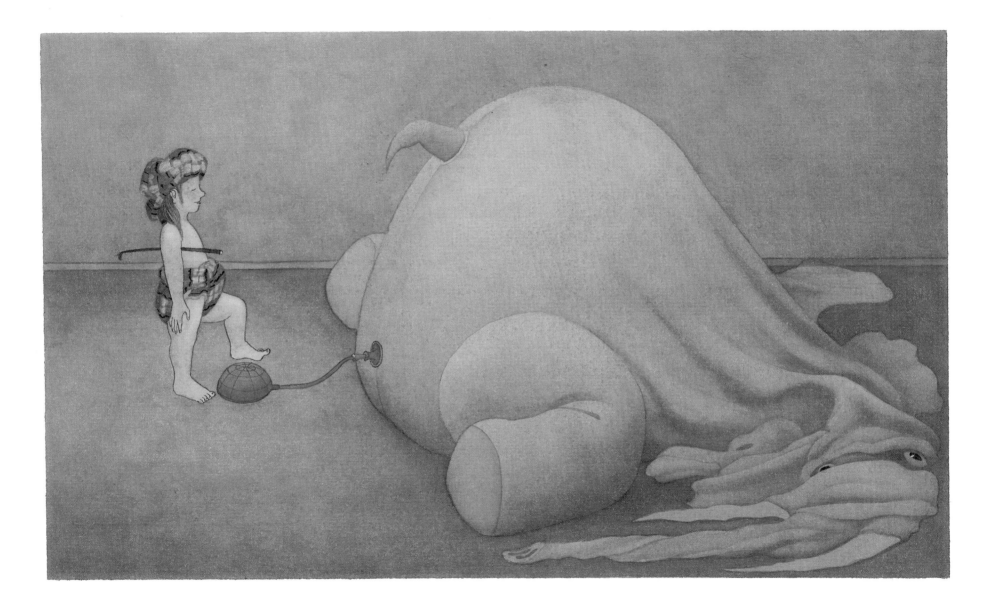

era won't share.

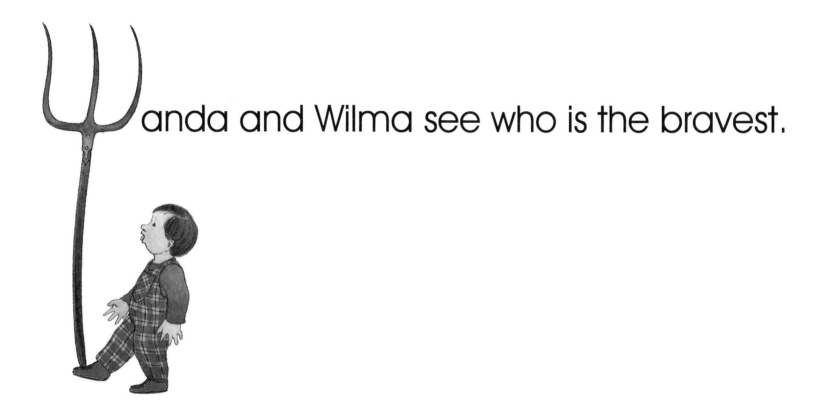

anda and Wilma see who is the bravest.

Beatri  bids everyone farewell.

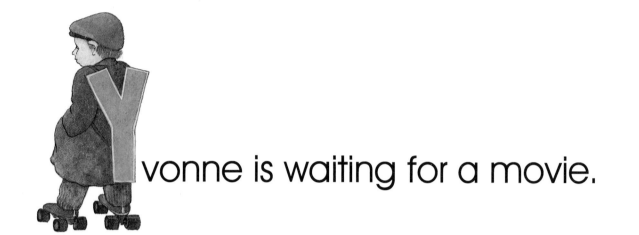vonne is waiting for a movie.

Zelda discovers the aeroport.